Shark
Feels Shy

CW00796805

Franklin Watts
First published in Great Britain in 2021 by Hodder & Stoughton

Copyright © Hodder & Stoughton Limited, 2021

All rights reserved.

Credits
Series Editor: Sarah Peutrill
Series Designer: Sarah Peden

Every attempt has been made to clear copyright. Should there be any
inadvertent omission please apply to the publisher for rectification.

ISBN: 978 1 4451 7453 2 (hardback)
ISBN: 978 1 4451 7454 9 (paperback)

Printed in China

MIX
Paper | Supporting
responsible forestry
FSC® C104740

Franklin Watts
An imprint of
Hachette Children's Group
Part of Hodder & Stoughton
Carmelite House
50 Victoria Embankment
London EC4Y 0DZ

An Hachette UK Company
www.hachette.co.uk

www.hachettechildrens.co.uk

THE Emotion OCEAN

Shark
Feels Shy

by Katie Woolley and David Arumi

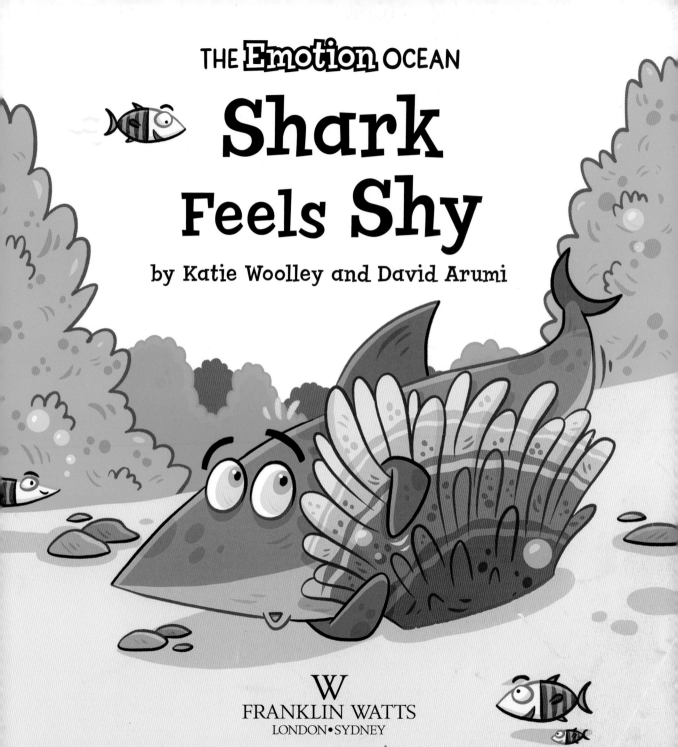

W
FRANKLIN WATTS
LONDON•SYDNEY

It was Friday afternoon and time for Class One's show and tell.

Everyone was very excited.
Well, almost everyone ...

Shark had been quiet all day. He had brought in his pet but he didn't want to stand in front of the class on his own.

"Who wants to go first?" asked Mr Narwhal.

Whale raised her flipper up and bounced on her tail fin.

"Me! Me!" she sang.

Whale read a lovely poem.

Angelfish showed a colourful picture.

Swordfish and Jellyfish danced together.

Then it was Shark's turn. Shark swam up to the teacher's desk.

12

But when he turned to look out at his friends, his tummy did a *BIG* somersault.

"Um, this is my ... I, I, I ..." he stammered.

Suddenly, Shark swam away.

Mr Narwhal hunted everywhere for Shark. He found him in the lost property cupboard.

"I can't do it," sniffed Shark. "I don't like everyone looking at me. I feel shy."

"It's OK to feel shy," said Mr Narwhal.
"Everyone feels shy sometimes."

"I want to show everyone Sid but not on my own," he said sadly.

Mr Narwhal had an idea.

Class One was waiting for Shark.

"Are you OK?" asked Starfish.

"Yes!" grinned Shark. "I felt shy but Mr Narwhal has an idea. Will you help me?"

Everyone in Class One thought Mr Narwhal's idea was great.

"It's the perfect end to our show and tell!" cried Jellyfish.

The whole class stood up. Shark began to uncoil Sid.

Shark took a deep breath. "This is Sid. He's my best friend," he whispered. Then, in a clear, loud voice he said, "He's a sea snake!"

Shark looked at all his friends standing next to him.

Suddenly Shark didn't feel shy anymore.
His tummy didn't do a somersault.

Shark felt **brave!**

Hiss!

Emotions are BIG!

Your feelings are a big part of you, just like they are a big part of Shark and his friends. Look at the pictures and talk about these feelings. Here are some questions to help you:

Were all the animals of Class One excited about show and tell?

Why did Shark swim away?

What did Shark do
to help him stop
feeling shy?

How did Shark feel at
the end of the story?

Can you think of a time
when you have felt shy?

We all feel shy sometimes,
even grown ups! Ask a
grown up if they can tell
you when they have felt
shy, too.

Let's Talk About Feelings

The Emotion Ocean series has been written to help young children begin to understand their own feelings, and how those feelings and subsequent actions affect themselves and others.

It provides a starting point for parents, carers and teachers to discuss BIG feelings with little learners. The series is set in the ocean with a class of animal friends who experience these big emotions in familiar, everyday scenarios.

Shark Feels Shy

This story looks at feeling shy, how it makes you feel, how you react to the feeling of being shy and how you can help overcome the emotion and begin to feel brave.

The book aims to encourage children to identify their own feelings, consider how feelings can affect their own happiness and the happiness of others, and offer simple tools to help manage their emotions.

How to use the book

The book is designed for adults to share with either an individual child, or a group of children, and as a starting point for discussion.

Choose a time when you and the children are relaxed and have time to share the story.

Before reading the story:

• Spend time looking at the illustrations and talking about what the book might be about before reading it together.

• Encourage children to employ a 'phonics-first' approach to tackling new words by sounding them out.

After reading the story:

• Talk about the story with the children. Ask them to describe Shark's feelings. Ask them if they have ever felt shy. Can they remember when and why?

• Ask the children why they think it is important to understand their feelings. Does it make them feel better to understand why they feel the way they do in certain situations? Does it help them get along with others?

• Place the children into groups. Ask them to think of a scenario when somebody might feel shy. What do their friends do to make them feel better? (For example, ask them to play, or sit with them if they are upset.)

• At the end of the session, invite a spokesperson from each group to read out their list to the others. Then discuss the different lists as a whole class.